Samuel French Acting Edition

Off Off Broadway Festival Plays 43rd Series

Rabiosa
by Nelson Diaz-Marcano

The Forgotten Place
by Jeff Locker

Baked Goods
Book by Charlie Cohen
Music by Helen Park
Lyrics by Christyn Budzyna

Ballgirl
by Gracie Gardner

Better
by Vince Gatton

The Ferberizing of Coral
by Patrick Flynn

SAMUELFRENCH.COM   SAMUELFRENCH.CO.UK

ISBN 978-0-573-70777-3

www.SamuelFrench.com
www.SamuelFrench.co.uk

FOR PRODUCTION ENQUIRIES

UNITED STATES AND CANADA
Info@SamuelFrench.com
1-866-598-8449

UNITED KINGDOM AND EUROPE
Plays@SamuelFrench.co.uk
020-7255-4302

Each title is subject to availability from Samuel French, depending upon country of performance. Please be aware that *OFF OFF BROADWAY FESTIVAL PLAYS 43RD SERIES* may not be licensed by Samuel French in your territory. Professional and amateur producers should contact the nearest Samuel French office or licensing partner to verify availability.

No one shall make any changes in this title(s) for the purpose of production. No part of this book may be reproduced, stored in a retrieval system, or transmitted in any form, by any means, now known or yet to be invented, including mechanical, electronic, photocopying, recording, videotaping, or otherwise, without the prior written permission of the publisher. No one shall upload this title(s), or part of this title(s), to any social media websites.

For all enquiries regarding motion picture, television, and other media rights, please contact Samuel French.

MUSIC USE NOTE

Licensees are solely responsible for obtaining formal written permission from copyright owners to use copyrighted music in the performance of this play and are strongly cautioned to do so. If no such permission is obtained by the licensee, then the licensee must use only original music that the licensee owns and controls. Licensees are solely responsible and liable for all music clearances and shall indemnify the copyright owners of the play(s) and their licensing agent, Samuel French, against any costs, expenses, losses and liabilities arising from the use of music by licensees. Please contact the appropriate music licensing authority in your territory for the rights to any incidental music.

IMPORTANT BILLING AND CREDIT REQUIREMENTS

If you have obtained performance rights to this title, please refer to your licensing agreement for important billing and credit requirements.

The Samuel French Off Off Broadway Short Play Festival (OOB) has been the nation's leading short play festival for forty-three years. The OOB Festival has served as a doorway to future success for aspiring writers. Over 200 plays have been published, and many participants have become established, award-winning playwrights.

For more information on the Samuel French Off Off Broadway Short Play Festival, including history, interviews, and more, please visit www.oobfestival.com.

Festival Artistic Director: Casey McLain
Literary Coordinator: Garrett Anderson
Editorial Coordinator: Sarah Weber
Production Coordinators: Coryn Carson, Carly Erickson
Marketing Team: Lawrence Haynes, Alejandra Venancio, Chris Kam, Courtney Kochuba, Ryan Pointer
Festival Publicity Director: Abbie Van Nostrand
Stage Manager: Jane Silverstein
House Manager: Tyler Mullen
Box Office Manager: Rosemary Bucher
Announcer: Coryn Carson
Festival Staff: Samantha Cooper, Sean Demers, Kate Karcewzski, Zach Kaufer, Fiona Kyle, Marilin Matos, Nicole Matte, Elizabeth Minski, Charlie O'Leary, Rachel Smith, Ali Tesluk, Amy Rose Marsh

HONORARY GUEST PLAYWRIGHT
Charles Busch

FESTIVAL JUDGES
John M. Baker
Nan Barnett
Ken Cerniglia
Kirsten Childs
B.J. Evans
Chris Giordano
Adam Greenfield
David Greenspan
Hansol Jung
Lisa Rothe
Max Vernon
Susan Westfall

TABLE OF CONTENTS

Foreword..7

Rabiosa...9
by Nelson Diaz-Marcano

The Forgotten Place...21
by Jeff Locker

Baked Goods 35
Book by Charlie Cohen
Music by Helen Park
Lyrics by Christyn Budzyna

Ballgirl.. 49
by Gracie Gardner

Better.. 59
by Vince Gatton

The Ferberizing of Coral...................................... 73
by Patrick Flynn

FOREWORD

Samuel French is honored to have the eight daring and inspirational playwrights included in this collection as the winners of our 43rd Annual Off Off Broadway Short Play Festival. This year our Festival received over 800 submissions from around the world. We thank all of these gifted playwrights for sharing their talent with us and welcome each writer into our elite group of Off Off Broadway Festival winners.

We also wish to thank the producing companies who helped stage these works at our Festival. The vital relationship between playwright and theatre is one that we know well at Samuel French. Whether producing a Tony-winning play or developing a new work, theatre companies play a vital role in cultivating new audiences and communicating a playwright's vision. We commend them for this mission and thank each of the producers involved in the 43rd Annual Festival for their tireless dedication and contributions to their playwright.

Perhaps the most challenging part of the OOB Festival is our production week. From our initial pool of Top Thirty playwrights, we ultimately select six plays for publication and representation by Samuel French. Of course, we can't make our selection alone, so we enlist some brilliant minds within the theatre industry to help us in this process. Each night of the Festival, we have an esteemed group of three judges consisting of a Samuel French playwright and two other members of the theatre industry. We thank them for their support, insight, and commitment to the art of playwriting.

Samuel French is a 189-year-old company rich in history while at the same time dedicated to the future. We are constantly striving to develop groundbreaking methods that will better connect playwright and producer. With a team committed to continuing our tradition of publishing and licensing the best new theatrical works, we are boldly embracing our role in this industry as bridge between playwright and theatre.

On behalf of our board of directors; the entire Samuel French team in our New York, Los Angeles, and London offices; and the over 10,000 playwrights, composers, and lyricists that we publish and represent, we present you with the six winning plays of the 43rd Annual Samuel French Off Off Broadway Short Play Festival.

Get ready to be inspired.

Casey McLain
Artistic Director
The Samuel French Off Off Broadway Short Play Festival

Rabiosa

Nelson Diaz-Marcano

RABIOSA premiered as part of the 43rd Annual Samuel French Off Off Broadway Short Play Festival at the Vineyard Theatre in New York City on August 21, 2018. The director was Victoria Collado. The cast was as follows:

ROCIO .... Guadalis Del Carmen

CHARACTERS

ROCIO – (twenties–forties) Latinx female

SETTING

Cabo Rojo, Puerto Rico

TIME

September 23, 2017
a few days after Hurricane Maria devastated the island

(At rise: There's nothing onstage until **ROCIO** *comes running in. She is literally fury!)*

ROCIO. Oye! Mira tu Cabrona! Stop right there.

(She takes an imaginary lasso and throws it at the Hurricane. Doesn't catch her.)

Todavia te veo pendeja! I can still see that damn tail of yours, Maria! You think you slick!

(You can feel the wetness in the air.)

You think you can come here, to my house, and leave a mess! Look at it.

(She looks around.)

Oh man, you took away Don Rafa's house? That's some shit, I didn't even realize it was gone.

(She takes a second.)

I used to love going to visit there. Rafa is a cool old man... Fuck Maria, where am I gonna buy my chicles now when I'm at the beach? Ah, did you ever think about that? No you didn't. You didn't give a fuck. I know. My grandma told me about it. After we dodged Irma, she said to me, "That other one, she is spiteful. I hear it."

(Beat.)

The spirits told her. Yeah that's right the spirits, and they didn't have anything good to say about you. None of them. That's what she told me anyway.

(She throws the lasso again.)

Almost! Stay still! This is the lasso she gave me to get you in case you thought of running away. There's a lot you got to answer to! Like for example, do you know how long it took me to get to the beach?

(She waits for an answer.)

A long ass time, oíste. You left all the roads pelaos, and the trees all over the floor. Couldn't use my car for shit. Who does that? The little road I used to take to school by the creek looks like somebody just took a deep dump on it. Just mud all over with cuanta porqueria flew its way. I used to sit in a tree branch by it and eat jobos, but guess what happened to the tree? Yes, you fucking took it!

(She throws the lasso again.)

I'm getting close, you getting scared. You know why I loved that tree so much? No you didn't even ask anybody if you could take it, you just came and took everything you wanted without consideration. Was this your manifest destiny? Don't you know we already have a debt the size of Russia? Actually did you take the debt with you? Nah you left that here. 'Cause you's a bitch!

(Beat. She starts prepping herself to throw the lasso again.)

You know that tree was where my grandma used to speak to the spirits?! She said when she was younger it was easier to see them. Most people had a connection with them. She being one of them. They are the ones who gave her this lasso, so she could play. They had some crazy games. She said you could only hear them if you put your ear to the sand. And if you don't hear them, speak to them. Read them poetry. Abuela had her thing, but I believed her as much as I could.

(She throws the lasso again. And fails.)

She said the magic left the more Americanized we became. That the bays used to light up with the touch, and that you could hear them play at night around the house. She still heard them a few days ago, but she said their voices were faint, and that the warning was clear. This was our last stand. Whose? I don't know, but did you take them too?

(She tries again and nothing. She gets really frustrated.)

Coño! Be brave and come answer for your sins. If I can come all the way from New York City, you can come all the way back. You made me so worried about Grandma I came to stay with her. And guess what? Guess what always been my favorite thing about coming back home? That you could hear the coquis at night and the roosters in the morning, the island's own soundtrack. That's the kind of magic I grew up with. The kind of magic we are still allowed to have. Guess what I heard last night?

(Beat.)

Nothing. And this morning? Nothing... Just dread. Just pain. Just neighbors trying to find what they lost of themselves in the same paths we all became people. All of them trying to look at each other and give some support. It was the first time a half-smile had to do for boricuas. We never half-smile. We either smile oreja a oreja, or yell at you. That half-smile shit, that ain't us. But it was today.

(She takes a second.)

These are the same people I used to spend the nights with. In the little shack behind Joselito's house, we used to play dominoes with the viejos. Get a pork, get it done. Get some frias and put some music and ya. Dance and talk shit all night. Smile and stumble till the sun rose up. Listening to the coquis then seeing them hide when the gallos *[rooster sound]*. We used to come to Rafa's place there and ask him to tell us stories. And he would. Viejo verde, once the girls started developing we had to stop going. But he never did anything, just look too much. I still went. Nothing to go now. You took Joselito's shack too, at least half. So no parties either. Juts half-smiles and...

(She stays silent.)

My grandma told me to go back, that this would be the end. The last breath was coming. The spirits were afraid. The last of the taino essence would be gone. She said Irma was a warning, but we didn't realize it. That you, you were angry. That this is what happens when the magic is finally gone. I haven't gone to the bay that lights up yet, but I bet it may not even light up anymore. Fuck that!

(She takes the lasso and throws it.)

Come here!

(She throws it again.)

Talk to me!

(Picks up the lasso.)

I am the spawn of Goyo Mercado y Tati! The descendant of my abuelos! I'm from the little island that produced giants like Clemente and Albizu, of Rita Moreno and Julia de Burgos. I am a combination of the Taino, the white man and the black warrior! I come from being taken over and over yet never stopping being who I am. I am from the island Borinquen, goddamn it and you ain't shit!

(She cackles.)

Escuchaste! You ain't shit. I know shit. I met Ricky Martin once. Well more like he wave at me from afar. And by me, I mean the crowd, but still. Our eyes locked. He is shit, and you ain't. You think you got us. Ha!

(She starts laughing until she sobs, ever so slightly.)

Cabrona! Come back. Bring back Rafa's house, and Joselito's shack and my tree. Bring back the lights on the bay and the lives you took. Bring back my grandmother! Bring her back!

(She throws the lasso.)

We don't have much time! My cousin will be burying her today, she is starting to smell and nobody is able to come pick up her body. But I know it's just the spirits trying to keep her there till she comes back. But you took her. You took her away. And now my cousin is preparing to bury her by Joselito's shack. How could you do this? How can you continue to move and leave us like this!

> *(She throws the lasso one more time and watches it fall, then in anger throws it to the floor.)*

Porqueria! What good is a magic lasso if it doesn't work! Maybe she is right; maybe this was Puerto Rico's last stand...

> *(She sits on the floor. The sound of wind is heard. Suddenly she decides to put her ear to the ground. No sound. She knocks.)*

No pulse.

> *(She starts doing CPR pushes on the sand, or Puerto Rico's chest.)*

Vamos Puerto Rico!

> *(She keeps going.)*

Vamos puñeta!

> *(She keeps going and pushing, but nothing. Then she starts banging it in frustration. Suddenly she breaks down and sits down. Then smiles as if she thought of something. She puts her ear to the ground. She looks for a book she has with Julia De Burgos poems.)*

¡Cómo quiere tumbarme esta carga de siglos
que en mi espalda se bebe la corriente del tiempo!
Tiempo nunca cambiante que en los siglos se estanca
y que nutre su cuerpo de pasados reflejos.

*(She puts her ear to the ground...nothing. Her
face shows frustration.)*

Tengo miedo de lo alto de tus miras – me dice –;
el ayer que me nutre se doblega en lo interno
de tu vida sencilla, que no admite pasado,
y que vive en lo vivo desplegada al momento;
ya me enfada la siempre desnudez de tu mente
que repele mi carga y se expande en lo nuevo;
ya me turba la fina esbeltez de tu idea
que flagela mi rostro y endereza tu cuerpo...
mira a un lado y a otro: jorobados, mediocres;
son los míos, los que abrevan mi vacío siempre lleno;
sé uno de ellos; destuerce tu vanguardia; claudica;
es tan fácil volcarse de lo vivo a lo muerto.

(She puts her ear down. Nothing.)

Coño!

Has querido tumbarme, carga en cuerpo de siglos
de prejuicios, de odios, de pasiones, de celos.

*(She puts her ear down again, nothing. With
her ear to the ground she recites the next.)*

Has querido tumbarme con tu carga pesada,
mas al punto encontréme y fue vano tu empeño.

*(Nothing. We see her face just giving up.
Suddenly, a slight sound of a heart pounding.
She gets happy and quickly looks for the next
verse. She says it to Maria.)*

Vete, forra tus siglos con el vulgo ignorante;
no son tuyas mis miras; no son tuyos mis vuelos.

(The sound of the heart becomes louder.)

Soy en cuerpo de ahora; del ayer no sé nada.
En lo vivo mi vida sabe el Soy de lo nuevo.

(The heart now becomes a steady sound. Then she feels the spirits coming back inside of her. She gasps and trembles as they become one with her. A smile forms on her face.)

There, there, we ain't dead yet.

(She closes her eyes as the sound of the heartbeat overwhelms the stage.)

End of Play

The Forgotten Place

Jeff Locker

THE FORGOTTEN PLACE was produced as part of Strings at the Meta Theatre at Anthony Meindl's Actor Workshop on December 8, 2017. The director was Lindsay Frame. The cast was as follows:

ERIC . . . . .Jeff Locker
KIP . . . . Brian Flaccus

THE FORGOTTEN PLACE was produced as part of the 43rd Annual Samuel French Off Off Broadway Short Play Festival at the Vineyard Theatre in New York City on August 24, 2018. The director was Lindsay Frame. The cast was as follows:

ERIC . . . . .Jeff Locker
KIP . . . . Brian Flaccus

CHARACTERS

ERIC – thirty-six, male
KIP – thirty-three, male

SETTING

A small office in Anywhere, USA

TIME

Late afternoon

AUTHOR'S NOTES

Notes on Punctuation

Italics are pointedly emphasized.
ALL CAPS are loudly emphasized.
Slashes (/) indicate overlapping dialogue.

(We are in a small, minimalistic office. There is a desk with two chairs on each side, an unassuming lamp on the left side of the desk, a pot with one sunflower on the right, and two very neat stacks of papers in the middle. And nothing else.)

*(**ERIC** sits at the desk, nervously sorting through the papers. There's a knock at the door.)*

ERIC. Come in!

*(The door opens and a head belonging to **KIP** pops through the crack.)*

KIP. Eric?

ERIC. Kip?

KIP. Yep!

ERIC. You're in the right place!

*(He stands up, walks over, enthusiastically shakes **KIP**'s hand, then motions to the empty chair in front of his desk.)*

Have a seat!

KIP. Thanks!

(They both sit at the same time.)

ERIC. Did you have trouble getting here?

KIP. No, pretty easy to find, actually.

ERIC. Ah, if only everything in life were that easy to find, right?

KIP. So true. And thanks for responding. Most people don't. I mean, not that there's anything wrong with my resume or –

ERIC. *(Picks up the resume.)* Oh no, it looks great actually. Good schools, extra-currics, hobbies, pretty stable family life... Single? That's good.

KIP. Well that'll change, of course. But I don't want it to get in the way –

ERIC. *(Looks down at resume.)* Well unfortunately it does more often than not.

KIP. Yeah, no, I totally understand. Bentley, my last –

ERIC. *Bentley?*

KIP. Yeah I know, right?

ERIC. That guy didn't stand a chance, did he?

KIP. Nah he was a good guy, it's just, you know, he fell in love and his partner was really controlling.

ERIC. It takes work, and not everyone is up to the challenge.

KIP. That's why I'm here!

ERIC. Well I'm glad you applied!

> *(Smiles, looks at the resume, then back to* **KIP.***)*

So just so we're clear, you're here for the best friend position...

KIP. Oh, yeah, totally.

ERIC. Cuz I'm not looking for casual acquaintances or like *bros* or – I mean, not that those are bad or anything.

KIP. No, it just depends on where you are in life.

ERIC. *(Surprised and very pleased.)* Exactly! I'm so glad you get that. That's hugely important.

KIP. No, that's why when I saw your ad... Sometimes the job description is so vague and you just end up wasting each other's time and it's like, *what was the point of that?*

> *(They share a smile of mutual understanding.)*

ERIC. Cool well so far so good! I'm glad we're on the same page.

> *(Back to resume.)*

So I had some stuff I wanted to go over, if that's okay.

KIP. Oh absolutely.

ERIC. Awesome.

(Looks at resume.)

So, tell me about "Kip."

KIP. Named after the main character in a children's book. *The Mystical, Magical, Mythical Journey to the Forgotten Place.* You heard of it?

ERIC. No. But I'm going to get you an autographed copy for your thirty-fifth birthday.

KIP. I'm going to love that. Nice.

ERIC. I'm going to call you "Kipster," though.

KIP. Ha that's cool, just not when anyone else is around, yeah?

ERIC. Got it.

KIP. And "Eric"? Can I call you "Ear Ache"?

ERIC. No, my dad called me that as a kid and we don't get along.

KIP. Gotcha. I'll only use it once, at your dad's funeral, to make you laugh.

ERIC. I'll need a little snark from you that day.

KIP. Well I'll be good for some choice snark over the years.

ERIC. Thanks man.

KIP. That's what BFFs are for.

ERIC. Yeah we're not going to call each other BFFs though, but we'll know it nonetheless.

KIP. Oh yeah, we'll keep certain things unsaid for sure. But we'll...

ERIC & KIP. ...Always be there for each other. Hey!

ERIC. Totally!

(This is their first giddy WOW moment.)

This is going great!

KIP. Right?

ERIC. Best interview today!

KIP. Ah I'm so glad. But don't you think –

ERIC. We should cover some of the "less ideal personality quirks" stuff?

KIP. Yeah.

ERIC. Oh absolutely. So you should know I have anxiety and as it gets worse I'm going to end up canceling on a lot of stuff.

KIP. Anything important?

ERIC. Well, definitely a few BBQs, some dinners, and...your fortieth birthday party.

KIP. Oh shit, that sucks. I'm going to be really upset.

ERIC. But it'll only be because I'm going to have a panic attack outside the restaurant and won't be able to leave my car.

KIP. Fuck, that's going to hurt.

ERIC. I'm sorry. Once the panic attacks start it's going to really affect...a lot.

KIP. But I'm going to force you to see a therapist and take your ass to your first visit myself.

ERIC. And I'm going to pretend it's no big deal, but you'll never know how much that'll mean to me.

KIP. No, of course not. But it'll make our friendship stronger.

ERIC. Without a doubt. So much that I'm going to have really confusing feelings for you.

KIP. *(Blushes.)* Yeah.

ERIC. *(Thoroughly embarrassed.)* And one night when we're shit-faced –

KIP. You're going to kiss me.

ERIC. Yep! That's going to take a lot of courage on my part and scare the SHIT out of me.

KIP. But I'll let you because it's what you need. To let it out. Plus...

ERIC. Plus...

> *(Points to his bow tie.)*

...you'll have always kind of known.

KIP. Duh. You're my best friend. I'm not going to dump you because of a little kiss.

ERIC. But you will end up –

KIP. Setting you up with the love of your life.

ERIC. Yeah.

> *(They take a moment and breathe that in.)*

So...

KIP. So...

ERIC. We should talk about the –

KIP. Bad stuff.

ERIC. Yeah.

KIP. I'm going to be a bit of a dick on occasion.

ERIC. Yeah me too.

KIP. I'll conveniently miss some important texts.

ERIC. I'll go days without answering yours.

KIP. I'll call you clingy to my other friends.

ERIC. I'll *be* clingy.

KIP. I'll wonder if we should be friends anymore.

ERIC. I'll look for another friend.

KIP. I'm going to start drinking...a *lot*.

ERIC. I'm gonna go through a self-abusive anonymous hookup phase.

KIP. You're not going to tell me though.

ERIC. No, even after a guy rapes me.

KIP. Fuck.

ERIC. We'll be in a weird place by then, keeping all sorts of secrets from each other.

KIP. Yeah. I won't tell you about the cancer.

ERIC. What? No! Fuck.

KIP. Nah it'll just be a mole. I'll have it removed.

ERIC. Jesus, that would scare the hell out of me.

KIP. That's why I won't tell you. Plus I keep things inside.

ERIC. As you always will.

(He takes a deep breath as he prepares for what's next.)

ERIC. You're going to hurt me.

KIP. Eric...

ERIC. Bad.

KIP. I know.

ERIC. I'll get hit with depression and feel like I have no one /

KIP. And I'm going to make it worse /

ERIC. You're gonna say some awful things /

KIP. That you're clingy /

ERIC. We covered that /

KIP. That you're unstable /

ERIC. And /

KIP. And that you should just man up /

ERIC. And /

KIP. And get a fucking life /

ERIC. *(Stands up, faces* **KIP.***)* But you'll be such a big part of my life /

KIP. And I'll make fun of you /

ERIC. Betray me /

KIP. Behind your back /

ERIC. To the same guys who call me fag /

KIP. *(Rises, faces* **ERIC**, *indignant.)* They won't mean it /

ERIC. They'll *mean it* /

KIP. But I won't defend you /

ERIC. No you won't /

KIP. And you're going to try to guilt me into apologizing /

ERIC. I'll just want you to have my back /

KIP. You won't know the difference between me having your back and suffocating me /

ERIC. I'm going to have a breakdown. And you /

KIP. I'll pretend it never happened /

ERIC. And?

KIP. And what?

ERIC. And what will you do next?

KIP. I don't want to say it.

ERIC. You're in an interview. WE CAN'T GO FORWARD IF YOU CAN'T BE HONEST WITH ME.

KIP. Why do you need me to say it?

ERIC. BECAUSE IT'S PART OF THE PROCESS.

KIP. FUCK THE PROCESS!

ERIC. NO THE PROCESS IS EVERYTHING WE ARE NOTHING WITHOUT THE PROCESS THIS IS WORK THIS REQUIRES WORK! NOW TELL ME YOU FUCKER –

KIP. I'LL WISH I'D NEVER MET YOU! Okay? I'll wish we were never friends. I'll believe my life would've been better without you.

ERIC. And?

KIP. And don't.

ERIC. And?

KIP. And I'll tell you that. To your face. While you're more broken than ever.

ERIC. Yeah.

> *(They pause for a moment as they each take in the gravity of this, then sit.)*

KIP. I'll feel awful after.

ERIC. Me too.

KIP. And we won't talk.

ERIC. For years.

KIP. I'll get married. Have kids.

ERIC. Who I won't meet.

KIP. I'll try to reach out.

ERIC. I'll ignore you.

KIP. My son, Troy, will see a picture of you and ask.

ERIC. What will you say?

KIP. I'll say you were my best friend once.

ERIC. Oh. That's nice.

KIP. Well it's true. Even though we fucked it up.

ERIC. I'll realize I wasn't always easy to be friends with.

KIP. Yeah.

ERIC. I'll be so sad. Cuz I'm going to need you.

KIP. Me too.

ERIC. And we won't ever have –

KIP. Anyone like us again.

> *(They take a beat.* **ERIC** *leans forward toward* **KIP.***)*

ERIC. But I'll be there...

KIP. When I go?

ERIC. Yeah.

KIP. Stupid skin cancer.

ERIC. You should've told me.

KIP. I know.

ERIC. You should've told me.

KIP. I know.

ERIC. *(Crumbling.)* You should've told me.

KIP. I know.

> *(They can barely look at each other.)*

ERIC. *(Trying to be strong.)* Thank god Troy will call me.

KIP. He's going to be a good kid.

ERIC. He'll look so much like you.

KIP. Yeah.

ERIC. *(With a knowing twinkle in his eye.)* Gonna break some ladies' hearts.

KIP. More like some guys'.

ERIC. NO!

KIP. Yeah.

> *(They high five, delighted.)*

ERIC. Well all right.

KIP. I'll tell him if anything happens to me, you'll have his back.

ERIC. And I will.

KIP. I know.

>(**ERIC** *looks down at Kip's resume. It appears they've covered everything.*)

I'll know you're there.

ERIC. *(Not sure where this is going.)* Where?

KIP. At the hospital. When I go. I'll know you're there.

ERIC. You will?

KIP. Yeah.

ERIC. Really?

KIP. Yeah.

ERIC. That's good to know. You know?

KIP. I'll be so glad you're there.

ERIC. Yeah.

KIP. And hey.

ERIC. Yeah?

KIP. You're going to have a great life after I go.

ERIC. *(Immediately overcome with emotion.)* How will you know?

KIP. I just will.

ERIC. Yeah?

KIP. I mean, I'll know you. My best friend.

>(*They take each other in for a moment, spontaneously rise and embrace, then return to their seats. There is a long moment as they each sit with it all. They regain their composure and* **KIP** *leans back, looks at* **ERIC**.)

So, how'd I do?

>(**ERIC** *looks down at Kip's resume, then up to* **KIP**, *and gives him a warm, melancholic smile and a slight nod. Fade to black.*)

End of Play

Baked Goods

Book by Charlie Cohen

Music by Helen Park

Lyrics by Christyn Budzyna

BAKED GOODS premiered at the Sound Bites Festival on January 18, 2016. The show was also presented as part of City Theatre's Summer Shorts on June 1, 2017, and at the 43rd Annual Samuel French Off Off Broadway Short Play Festival at the Vineyard Theatre in New York City on August 21, 2018. The OOB performance was directed by Charlie Cohen, with choreography by Samantha Amaral and orchestrations by Collin Martin. The cast was as follows:

GERTIE .... Kelly Whitley

MAXWELL .... Steven Kane

TERRI .... Christine St. Pierre

CHARACTERS

GERTIE – a hapless but lovable eleven-year-old who wants to prove to her mom that she's worthy of being a Girl Scout

MAXWELL – a business-savvy eleven-year-old who longs to be a Girl Scout

TERRI – Gertie's no-nonsense mother and Girl Scout troop leader

CUSTOMER – (doubles as Terry) a stoner with a sweet tooth

Scene One

[MUSIC NO. 01 "GIRL SCOUT SONG"]

(San Francisco. Weaverville Recreational Center. The last Girl Scout meeting of the year.)

TERRI & GERTIE.

> I WILL DO MY BEST TO BE
> WHAT THE GIRL SCOUTS OF AMERICA EXPECT OF ME
> I'LL BE RESPONSIBLE FOR WHAT I SAY AND DO
> I'LL ALWAYS BE COURAGEOUS
> AND I WILL BE CARING TOO
> 'CAUSE KINDNESS IS CONTAGIOUS!
> AND I'LL ALWAYS REMEMBER
> TO STAND AND SHOUT,
> "I'LL BE A SISTER TO EVERY SCOUT!"

TERRI. Scouts, every year, we get the opportunity to do the greatest of good – selling cookies to America. You have done amazing sales and you all deserve the Cookie Badge you have received today. And it's possible that among us is a Girl Scout with the talent to break my unbroken regional sales record. Continue to strive for greatness! See you girls next year! Gertie. Another year without a badge?

GERTIE. I guess so, Mom.

TERRI. I worry about you all the time, Gertie. You don't seem to understand what it means to be a Girl Scout. I mean, you've never –

[MUSIC NO. 02 "NEVER WON A BADGE"]

*(She continues with her speech, mouthing silently, as **GERTIE** steps out and sings.)*

39

GERTIE.

>
I NEVER WON A BADGE
I TRIED TO WIN THE PET CARE BADGE
AND KILLED OFF ALL THE FISHES
I TRIED TO WIN THE COOKING BADGE
AND RUINED DADDY'S DISHES

>
I NEVER WON A BADGE
I TRIED TO WIN THE FIRST AID BADGE
AND GAVE THE GIRLS INFECTIONS
THE OTHERS WON THE HIKING BADGE
AND I LOST THE DIRECTIONS

>
GREAT-GRANDMA WON THE GOLD AWARD
FOR ALL HER VOLUNTEERING
AND GRANDMA ROSE KNIT SWEATERS
FOR THE SOLDIERS OFF AT WAR
AND MOM SOLD ALL THOSE COOKIES BACK IN NINETEEN
    EIGHTY-FOUR

TERRI. I worry about you. You have to shape up! I don't want you to end up like your uncle, that deadbeat doper.

GERTIE.

>
OH, BUT I NEVER WON A BADGE
I SEIZE AND HYPERVENTILATE
WITH EACH NEW EXPECTATION
AND ALL THE OTHERS TEASE ME FOR
MY LACK OF CONCENTRATION
I NEVER EVEN GOT THE ONE
FOR CLASS PARTICIPATION!

TERRI. Gertie, I said I'm missing your final sales sheet. Where is it?

>
*(**GERTIE** hands it over painfully.)*

Gertie? There isn't a single sale recorded here. What happened to all the cookies you were supposed to sell?

GERTIE. I...lost them?

TERRI. You lost fifty boxes?

GERTIE.

>
I ATE THEM!

I KNEW I SHOULDN'T
BUT I ATE THEM!
I COULDN'T HELP IT!
THE MOUNTAINS OF THIN MINTS
AND PILES OF PATTIES
AND TREFOIL TOWERS
ALL OVER THE PLACE
I STUFFED THEM ALL IN MY FACE!

TERRI. As troop leader, I'm expected to report this to Girl Scout Headquarters. Rules are rules. If you don't sell one hundred boxes by the end of the day, you won't be a Scout anymore. I'll be in the car.

GERTIE. I can't be a Girl Scout anymore?

I HAVE TO WIN A BADGE
I KNOW I'M NOT ARTISTIC
ACADEMIC, OR ATHLETIC
AT LEAST I HAVE TO SHOW HER
I'M NOT TOTALLY PATHETIC

Scene Two

MAXWELL. *(From inside a closet.)* Psssst!

GERTIE. Hello?

MAXWELL. You're going about this all wrong.

GERTIE. Who said that?

MAXWELL. That doesn't matter. What does matter is you need to sell a lot of cookies. You'll never sell a single Samoa with that attitude.

GERTIE. What are you doing in the closet?

MAXWELL. What do you think?

GERTIE. This is a Girl Scouts meeting; boys shouldn't be –

MAXWELL. Look, it's time to hit the bricks, hit the corners and start slinging some Savannah Smiles!

GERTIE. What are Savannah –

MAXWELL. Savannah Smiles! Sugar dusted lemon cookies... Available in all scouting regions except for the Northwest? Replaced the Prairie Pecan Pralines in 1993? What kind of Girl Scout are you?

GERTIE. Not a very good one.

MAXWELL. You should consider yourself lucky. My mom makes me go to Boy Scouts because it's what boys my age should do. I have to tie knots while my sister gets to sell cookies. "Boys don't sell cookies."

GERTIE. Being a Girl Scout isn't as easy as you think.

MAXWELL. It shouldn't feel hard. It should feel like breathing.

GERTIE. You heard her. I'll never sell any cookies and I'll never get any badges. I'm not supposed to be a Girl Scout.

MAXWELL. There are three simple rules to selling Girl Scout cookies: knowing your customer base, knowing your product, and charming the pants off of everyone you meet.

[MUSIC NO. 03 "THAT'S HOW YA SELL 'EM"]

YOU HAVE TO USE YOUR BRAINS
AND YOU HAVE TO USE YOUR HEART

'CAUSE IT'S MORE THAN SELLING COOKIES
IT'S AN ART

YOU'VE GOT TO THINK IT THROUGH
THE FOLKS YOU'RE SELLING TO
WHAT KIND OF COOKIE DO THEY SPEND THEIR DOUGH
    FOR?
'CAUSE ONCE YOU'RE IN THE KNOW
THEIR CASH WILL DO-SI-DO
INTO YOUR PALM, GERTIE!
THAT'S HOW YA SELL 'EM!
THAT'S HOW YA SELL 'EM!

YOU HAVE TO KNOW THE PRICE
THE SUGARS AND THE SPICE
THAT BAKERS BAKE THEM TWICE TO SEAL THE FLAVOR
AND THEN I GUARANTEE
YOU SAY, "THEY'RE GLUTEN-FREE"
THEY'LL EAT IT UP, GERTIE!
THAT'S HOW YA SELL 'EM!
THAT'S HOW YA SELL 'EM!

THEY'LL NEVER HAVE A GIRL SCOUT GUY
I'LL NEVER GET THE CHANCE TO TRY
BUT I CAN HELP YOU THROUGH IT
I KNOW THAT YOU CAN DO IT

JUST FOLLOW WHAT I SAY
AND LOOK YOUR BEST TODAY
AND YOU WILL SEE THE WAY THE COOKIE CRUMBLES
SO SELL YOUR STASH WITH STYLE
AND FLASH THAT GIRL SCOUT SMILE
AND BE YOURSELF.
AND BE LIKE ME, GERTIE!
THAT'S HOW YA SELL 'EM
THAT'S HOW YA

GERTIE.
    THAT'S HOW YA SELL 'EM
    THAT'S HOW YA SELL 'EM!

GERTIE & MAXWELL.
    THAT'S HOW YA SELL 'EM!

GERTIE. Will you help me? I can't end up like my uncle.

MAXWELL. I thought you'd never ask. Now, where can we go to unload these cookies?

GERTIE. Well, Britney has dibs on the church parking lot. And Julie owns the park. Debbie has covered the Shriners, Friars, and Masons!

MAXWELL. Looks like you've lost the cookie holy trinity, old people, old people, and old people.

GERTIE. No! Wait! I can think of some places we can sell. Follow me!

Scene Three

[MUSIC NO. 04 "COOKIES FOR SALE"]

(**GERTIE** and **MAXWELL** set up shop in front of a nursing home.)

GERTIE.

COOKIES FOR SALE!
THE DO-SI-DOS WILL THRILL YOU
'CAUSE THEY TASTE SO GOOD, THEY'LL KILL YOU!
WHEN YOU SIT DOWN TO ENJOY YOU
KNOW THE THIN MINTS WILL DESTROY YOU
IN A VERY TASTY WAY!
WHY IS NO ONE BUYING TODAY?
OH LOOK – THAT LADY'S CRYING

MAXWELL.

'CAUSE YOU REMINDED THEM OF DYING!
That was not the right sales pitch for your customer base!

(**GERTIE** and **MAXWELL** set up their wagon in front of a synagogue.)

GERTIE.

COOKIES FOR SALE!
THEY'RE SO TASTY – I'M JUST SAYING
NEED A BREAK FROM ALL THAT PRAYING?
'CAUSE I BETCHA EVEN NOAH
WOULD'VE LOVED A GOOD SAMOA
COME AND TREAT YOURSELF TODAY!
WHY ARE THEY ALL WALKING AWAY?
I BET THAT THEY'D ENJOY 'EM

MAXWELL.

YOU'LL HAVE MUCH BETTER LUCK WITH GOYIM
The cookies aren't kosher, Gertie! It's just rule number two: knowing your product.

(**GERTIE** and **MAXWELL** set up camp in front of an allergist's office.)

GERTIE.

> COOKIES FOR SALE!
> THEY MAY BE A LITTLE FATTY
> TRY THE PEANUT BUTTER PATTY!
> IT'S NUTRITIOUS AND DELICIOUS
> WELL, IT'S MAYBE NOT NUTRITIOUS
> BUT THE TASTE WILL MAKE YOUR DAY!
> WHY ARE THEY ALL RUNNING AWAY?
> OH LOOK, THAT GUY IS SNEEZING

MAXWELL.

> HE'S BREAKING OUT IN HIVES AND WHEEZING!
> You have to charm them, Gertie, not poison them!

GERTIE. I'll never sell a single box. Not a single box!

MAXWELL. I'm sorry, Gertie. Maybe you weren't meant to be a Girl Scout. We don't always get to be what we want.

> (*A* **CUSTOMER** *stumbles out of a car, followed by a cloud of smoke.*)

CUSTOMER. Are those Thin Mints?

MAXWELL. Yes they are. Do you want a box?

CUSTOMER. I want three, dude!

MAXWELL. Amazing! Gertie, take the woman's money.

GERTIE. What just happened?

MAXWELL. You made a sale.

GERTIE. I what?

MAXWELL. You sold a box of cookies.

GERTIE. I sold three boxes of cookies!

MAXWELL. Good job! But you still have to sell all these other boxes if you want your badge.

GERTIE. How am I gonna do that?

MAXWELL. Follow her!

GERTIE. What? Why?

MAXWELL. Maybe she can lead us to others just like her. Her richer, hungrier friends.

GERTIE. Hey, wait up!

> (*They arrive at the Green Cross Marijuana Dispensary.*)

MAXWELL. What is this place?

GERTIE. That smell…it's familiar… It smells just like my uncle… HE LOVES COOKIES! I know what this is – My uncle taught me all about it! This is it –

[MUSIC NO. 04A "COOKIES FOR SALE – PART 2"]

Customers, product – I just have to charm them!

GERTIE & MAXWELL.

COOKIES FOR SALE!
HEY YOU! YA GOT THE MUNCHIES?
TRY MY TRIPLE CHOCOLATE CRUNCHIES
YOU WANT SEVEN BOXES? GREAT!

MAXWELL.

DOWN TO EIGHTY-EIGHT!
I don't know what you're saying, but it's working!

GERTIE. Hey, check it, dudes.

WHEN YOU'RE IN YOUR BASEMENT BLAZIN'
YOU'LL THINK, DUDE, THESE ARE AMAZIN'
AND YOU'LL WISH THAT YOU BOUGHT MORE!

MAXWELL.

DOWN TO FIFTY-FOUR!

GERTIE.

WHEN YOU WANT A TRIP TO HEAVEN
IN A BOX OR TWO OR SEVEN
CALL YOUR COOKIE DEALER – ME!

MAXWELL.

DOWN TO TWENTY-THREE

GERTIE & MAXWELL.

THREE
TWO
ONE

TERRI. *Gertie!!* I've been driving all around town looking for you! What are you doing here with all these degenerates? Did your uncle put you up to this? I can smell him here!

GERTIE. Mom I did it! I sold all my cookies! I'm a real Girl Scout and I'm gonna have a real badge!

TERRI. NO YOU ARE NOT!! You used exploitation and shady business dealings to sell cookies to a bunch of drug addicts! You have besmirched the Girl Scout code and you are hereby banned! For life!

GERTIE. But Mom –

TERRI. This is for your own good. Maybe now you'll learn to take things seriously.

GERTIE. Mom, I –

TERRI. I don't want to hear it. I'm so disappointed in you.

GERTIE. Mommy, I'm sorry –

MAXWELL. In the Girl Scout of the USA charter section thirty-three line seven it says, "Scouts are permitted to sell to any persons regardless of their sex, creed, religion, or political association"; as long as they do not sell to other Scouts. Do any of these people look like Girl Scouts? You owe Gertie that badge.

GERTIE. No, Mom, I don't want it. I don't want any of this. You're right, I'm the world's worst Girl Scout and that's fine. I don't need it.

(*She takes the badge and hands it to* **MAXWELL**.)

Here you go. You deserve this and like, fifty more. You're the best Girl Scout I've ever met.

[MUSIC NO. 05 "NEVER WON A BADGE"]

MAXWELL. I finally won a badge!

GERTIE.

I DON'T HAVE TO WIN A BADGE
MY NEW FRIEND WON A BADGE TODAY
AND I HELPED HIM ACHIEVE IT
I'M NOT THE BEST, BUT THAT'S OKAY
I'M GREAT, AND I BELIEVE IT!

End of Play

Ballgirl

Gracie Gardner

BALLGIRL premiered as part of Queens Theatre's Park Plays on July 28, 2017. The director was Emma Miller. The cast was as follows:

MARCY... Patrice Bell

BALLGIRL was produced as part of the 43rd Annual Samuel French Off Off Broadway Short Play Festival at the Vineyard Theatre in New York City on August 23, 2018. The director was Skylar Fox. The cast was as follows:

MARCY... Lindsley Howard

CHARACTERS

MARCY

(**MARCY**, *a teenage ballgirl at Arthur Ashe Stadium, stands at the baseline of the court.*)

MARCY. Like most people, I'm usually worried:

- is there something on my face,
- will I be attacked,
- and have I already humiliated myself today and am I just waiting for someone to point it out to me.

Sometimes I'm worried that I have a mysterious cancer that makes me want to sleep too much and makes me drag my feet. I'm worried it is slowly killing me, and that it is also contagious and airborne, and spreads when I tell people I love them, so I try my best not to.

Right now I'm worried about those things but also other things. Like:

- will I miss a catch,
- will I throw poorly,
- is this famous tennis player going to throw his racket at me and I'll have anisocoria like David Bowie with one permanently engorged pupil for the rest of my life?

Mostly the last. I like to make lists because it gives me a sense of control and structure, some feeling like I can anticipate what's coming next. That's why I got into this. I'm psychic. And catching balls is a kind of clairvoyance. It's a gift. It's physics and geometry, smashed into intuition and reflex. And that's why the players scare me.

You never know when a famous athlete will decide to become a petulant child on the court – or totally by accident and chance – will suddenly and totally lose control. Of course there are rules. But rules protect no one. Like Venus and Lindsay Davenport. Do you know this story?

The Hindrance Rule: Inadvertent or Deliberate Event: A distraction occurring on-court may be ruled inadvertent (unintentional) or ruled deliberate. Inadvertent distractions may include the following:

- a ball rolling onto the court,
- a ball falling out of a pocket,
- a hat falling off,
- or a sound or exclamation from a player.

Venus was wearing beads in her hair back then. And a few of them fell out. The umpire called a let. A few more fell out, and the umpire took her point. Rackets get thrown and they don't call lets. But god forbid a bead fall out. She lost the match. Rules protect no one.

(She offers a ball to the player and throws it.)

I love looking around and seeing all these faces in the stadium, none of them are looking at me. It's a kind of invisibility.

(A tennis ball flies toward her; she miraculously catches it. She puts it in her pocket. The crowd goes wild. Her eyes widen.)

That's not good. That's not good at all. I wanted to catch it, but not *that* well. I caught it *too* well, and now everyone is looking at me. Everyone really is looking at me, they are suddenly aware of me. Before, I was just a part of the event, a sword carrier. Now people expect me to do things.

What do they want me to do? I don't know. I have this feeling that they are watching, waiting. I'm supposed to stand here. I'm not supposed to do anything else. I can look very professional. That's something I can do.

(She looks very stern.)

Now I've taken focus from this famous tennis player. He's looking at me.

He looked at me too long. He's mad. Oh, he's mad. Even his ponytail is mad. Now there is an increased risk that this tennis player *will* throw his racket at me. If he loses the game it will be my fault.

Wait! No. I'm wonderful. It is not my fault if he loses the game.

> *(She offers the ball, throws it. She watches him serve, he misses.)*

Okay now he's going to the other ballgirl for the ball. Even though he's on my side.

He's very mad.

The idea of a player throwing a racket at me has always been a little bit absurd.

A little abstract.

That doesn't *happen*.

That happens to YouTube kids or people who deserve it.

I don't deserve to be hit with a racket. I'm not here to be on TV. I'm an athlete.

I'm a tennis player. I trained for this. I missed going on Model UN. Do you know what kids do at Model UN? They have *sex*. Okay? And they hone their diplomacy strategies.

And those are two of my highest priorities in this moment. And instead, I'm gonna be hit in the head with a racket by ponytail man. "Sexiest Man in American Tennis."

Guess what. No one cares! Definitely not me. I don't think you're sexy. I find your magazine centerfold washboard abs actually kind of freakish.

I don't know why I qualified that.

No!

They are Scary Abs. You look like a Ninja Turtle. I am not here for that.

> *(She offers the ball. He declines.)*

Fine. I don't want to give you my ball. You narcissist. I'm gonna look at your ponytail so hard you're gonna feel it. You're gonna feel my eyeballs burning into that gross tail. I'm sending fire-hot beams of rage at that silky pony.

How dare you look at me like that after my sick catch. That was a sick catch, friend. Have you ever had such a sick catch?

I bet he was never a ballkid.

He probably had sex. And he didn't need Model UN to do it.

He probably had bros.

Who would die for him.

I don't think anyone would die for me.

Maybe people would die for me if I played soccer. But I never wanted to do soccer. I wanted to play tennis. Singles Tennis. Probably because I didn't want anyone to die for me. Because I don't want to die for anyone else.

Why did I think being a ballgirl was a good idea? I sunk a tremendous amount of time and effort into this. When I could have just been playing tennis. Instead, I'm standing here, being paid almost nothing, to stand *around the tennis*. Looking *at the tennis*. I say I do it so I can see up-close but come on, I could be at home watching it on TV, instant replays on the couch.

I'm very good at this. Clearly. And now, everyone in this stadium has witnessed it. And the people who didn't witness it because they were in the bathroom or eating pretzels or zoning out, they feel bad. They missed out. They asked, "What happened?" And people were like, "Shhh, you missed it."

Because of me. People missed out because of something I did. That I don't even enjoy doing. Why would I torture myself by getting into this position? ...I must *enjoy* pain. I'm gonna grow up to be one of those kinky adults that are so embarrassing.

Wait.

No.

Sadomasochists make scrapbooks. They don't play tennis. I'm a tennis girl. I'm a ballgirl. I'm normal. I'm a normal-ass girl.

I'm a normal-ass girl.

(She offers the ball. She throws it.)

I'm a normal-ass girl.

I'm a:

- normal-ass girl who
- is a ballgirl at the U.S. flippin' Open who
- worked her ass off to get here and
- it is a miraculous honor to be here.

(She stands, absolutely unremarkably, doing her job, not posing or posturing. She catches the ball – efficient, invisible. Then, slowly, she lifts her shirt, exposing her stomach, which has the word "Applause" written across it in Sharpie. The crowd does.)

End of Play

Better

Vince Gatton

BETTER premiered as part of the 43rd Annual Samuel French Off Off Broadway Short Play Festival at the Vineyard Theatre in New York City on August 23, 2018. The director was Miller Hall. The cast was as follows:

RUTH. . . . . Nicole Naffaa
DONNA . . . . Erin Layton

CHARACTERS

RUTH – a middle-aged white woman who works at the plant
DONNA – a middle-aged white woman who works at the plant

SETTING

A workstation along the production line of a poultry processing plant, somewhere in Arkansas

TIME

Present day

(Two middle-aged white women stand working on the production line at a chicken processing plant in Arkansas. They wear white coveralls, hair coverings that look like shower caps, and protective eyewear. They each hold a pair of custom shears in their gloved hands, trimming excess fat and other tissue off the rough cuts of raw poultry that come down the line before sending them onward to be packaged.)

(Both women will stay busy working with their shears throughout the play.)

(They are not young. They are not quiet. Their sound is pure Ozarks.)

RUTH. So Wayne comes up to me –

DONNA. *That* a-hole.

RUTH. – That asshole comes up to me, and he says to me, "Ruth, would you mind if I gave you a little suggestion?"

DONNA. He did not!

RUTH. Oh, he did.

DONNA. That a-hole.

RUTH. So I look at this asshole and I'm thinking *I'm gonna suggest you eat shit in a second*, but also I just *gotta* hear this first, so what I say is, I say, "Why no, Wayne, by all means, suggest away." And he starts goin' on and on...I swear to god...about my elbows.

DONNA. Your elbows?

RUTH. I shit you not. He starts talking about my goddamned *elbows*. He's telling me how if I hold my elbows in, change my *stance* or whatever, I'll find that I'm much more *efficient*. Work faster and you know, *better*, cleaner movements and all.

DONNA. You've got to be kidding me.

RUTH. *Ergonomics* or whatever.

DONNA. That a-hole.

RUTH. And I'm thinkin', I know this isn't the hardest job in the goddamn world, you know, not the most *intellectually challenging* thing in the universe, but come on now, I'm not *stupid*. They took me off nights after just two years –

DONNA. – I know –

RUTH. – Just *two years* when it normally takes people at least five –

DONNA. – It took me five –

RUTH. – Because they noticed that, I don't know, I had half a brain or something, that the light in my eyes didn't come in through my goddamned ears. Five years on nights'll kill anyone with an IQ above ten.

DONNA. Now, I was on nights for –

RUTH. And THAT was two years before this motherfucker even worked here! And you know, when they moved me to first shift, they started askin' me about maybe bein' interested in workin' in that office up there, you know, in some kind of supervisory job or something –

DONNA. I know.

RUTH. Like they *identified* something in me or something, which I can tell you what it was, it was no great *hurdle* or nothin', it was having two fuckin' brain cells to rub together, that's all. Low bar, you know? But it is what it is around here, and around here that was e-goddamn-nough.

DONNA. ...

RUTH. But like, I'm gonna work up there in that office? Come on, now. Me? I just don't have the aptitude, you know? Or hell, no, fuck that: I have the goddamned *aptitude*, what I don't have is the goddamned *patience*. I couldn't put on a collared shirt every day, and some *slacks*, or hell, a goddamn *skirt*, and sit at a desk or

some shit – can you picture that? Me every day in a
fuckin' *skirt*?

DONNA. No.

RUTH. Right?? It's just...nah. I'm fine where I am. I don't
have kids, Henry's daughter was all grown before
I came along, so now there's nobody but myself to take
care of. This suits me just fine.

Nevertheless, I'm not some *rube*. And this asshole
comes along like I just fell off the fuckin' turnip truck,
and he's all giving me *suggestions*?

DONNA. He ain't never even worked this part of the line
anyway, what the heck does he know?

RUTH. I mean, this shit ain't brain surgery, what the hell
is he talkin' about? My *elbows*? This pissant is standin'
here trying to *educate* me about my fuckin' *elbows*?

DONNA. So what'd you do?

RUTH. I looked right at him and I said, "Why, thank you,
Wayne, that is indeed a helpful hint. Now can I give
you a suggestion? Why don't you go right ahead and
fuck off before I stick my elbows where the sun don't
shine."

DONNA. Ha!

RUTH. I said, "Look, with all due deference ya piece of shit,
don't tell me how to do my damn job."

DONNA. You did, didn't you?

RUTH. I damn well did. And then he gets all flustered and,
"Now, Ruth" this and that and I'm all, "No, sir, excuse
the fuck out a me, but no. I been doin' this a long time,
OK, and you may know a thing or two about *something*,
but it ain't *this*. So thank you very much, but I'll just
keep holdin' my goddamn elbows as I goddamn please."

DONNA. Speak of the devil...

*(She gestures with her chin and they look up
and out, toward the stairs going up to the
plant offices. Wayne has apparently appeared
there. They nod and wave, smiling.)*

RUTH. Piece of shit.

DONNA. That a-hole.

(*They return to their work.*)

So, Troy's back.

RUTH. Damn, Donna, that's right! How's he doin'?

DONNA. He's doin' great, glad to be home.

RUTH. Well, you must be relieved.

DONNA. I am, I am. He's finally done-done, no more deployments, back for good this time.

RUTH. Well, that's nice, I'm happy for you.

DONNA. We had a whole thing for him on Saturday, we cooked out and stuff. The cousins all came, we had like, banners and balloons and crap. It was fun.

RUTH. Well, good.

(*Beat.*)

DONNA. Mostly.

RUTH. Wait – did he bring that girl?

DONNA. Mmm-hmm.

RUTH. Tracey – no Stacey. Stacey, right? Stacey.

DONNA. Stacia.

RUTH. Stacia?

DONNA. Stacia.

RUTH. Well OK. *Stacia.*

DONNA. Yup.

RUTH. So what do you think?

DONNA. She's...different.

RUTH. Uh-oh.

DONNA. She called me "ma'am."

RUTH. Oh.

DONNA. Yeah.

RUTH. Oh, hell no.

DONNA. Yeah.

OK, so for one thing, she got real nice hair.

RUTH. Huh.

DONNA. *Real* nice. And there's a lot of it, too, like, you-gotta-spend-a-lotta-time-on-it hair.

And I kind of step back to get a good look at her, and that's when I see the boots. She got on these...boots, these shiny new boots, they come up way high –

RUTH. Well, la-di-da!

DONNA. – And this little outfit, I mean I wish I could even *explain* this outfit. A little skirt and a *blouse* or whatever, and it's a *cookout*, you know what I'm sayin'? We're havin' a dang cookout, I'm in my flip-flops and she's standing there all, "So nice to meet you, *ma'am*" in her shiny new boots and her nice clean clothes and I'm thinking, "What is this bullpoop?"

RUTH. So what'd you say?

DONNA. I don't say nothing. 'Cause a Troy. I just wanna be glad he's back and all. But dang if you can't barely even talk to him she's keeping so close, all up in everything.

So I finally do get him to myself in the kitchen for a half-second – and by the way, I can see out the window she ain't talkin' to nobody, can't be bothered, just sitting there in a chair all by herself like she's queen or something, everybody keepin' their distance – and all he wants to talk about is her. He tells me she's applyin' for a job here. At the plant. And I'm like, "Aw, heck." I can't even picture it, you know?

RUTH. Where the hell else is there, though?

DONNA. Right, I know, but *ugh*. She's the last thing I want to see every dang day – but like you said, where the heck else you gonna find a decent job around here? And then I start thinkin', sure, get her tush in here, that'll knock the fancy out of her quick enough.

RUTH. She'll be on nights for a good long while anyways...

DONNA. Right? So I go back out and I'm tryin' to be *welcoming*, I really am, and she tells me her interview's today – I mean, she said, "Monday," but it's today is my point – anyway, I'm lookin' at her and it's real clear she ain't never done a job like this before.

RUTH. I'm guessin' not.

DONNA. So I decide to be nice, 'cause dang it Troy likes her and I'm a Christian and I decide to be *nice*, and I tell her, well, I can help you learn the ropes or whatever, get...you know...

RUTH. Acclimated.

DONNA. ...Settled in or whatever. So I start givin' her some of the lowdown on what to say and who you gotta kinda kiss up to...but she doesn't really...she...she starts lookin' at Troy kinda funny and not sayin' anything. And finally *he's* the one that tells me.

RUTH. Tells you what?

DONNA. "No, Mama, she's not gettin' a job on the *floor*. She's tryin' for a job up in that office."

>   *(Beat.)*

RUTH. Well.

DONNA. And here's the part that sorta burns me up a little bit: he kinda *laughed* when he said it.

RUTH. ...Damn.

DONNA. Anyways. She thinks she's a secretary or something.

RUTH. ...

DONNA. Thinks she's something.

>   *(Beat. **RUTH** glances up toward the office.)*

RUTH. Speak of the devil...?

>   *(She gestures for **DONNA** to look.)*

DONNA. That's her, all right.

>   *(They pause their work, taking in the sight of Stacia climbing the stairs to the office for her interview.)*

RUTH. Damn, that is a lot a hair.

DONNA. Did I lie?

RUTH. No you did not.

DONNA. Can you see those boots, those goshdanged boots?

(**RUTH** *lifts her protective eyewear and squints.*)

RUTH. Damn.

DONNA. I know.

RUTH. Shiny.

DONNA. I KNOW.

(*They both react to something.*)

RUTH. OOP!

DONNA. Oh!

RUTH. Oooh! Oooh! Ya see that?

DONNA. Ha!

RUTH. She tripped *right* up that step!

DONNA. Oh, lord…!

RUTH. And of course there's goddamn Wayne…

DONNA. It's them boots! She can't even walk in 'em boots!

RUTH. She seems a little shaky… She OK, ya think?

DONNA. Just playin' it up to Wayne is all. See? She's fine.
Wear shoes you can walk in, dumbass.

(*She lets out a humorless little laugh.*)

And you know what? Danged if that isn't the same
dang outfit she was wearin' at the cookout. That is the
exact same blouse, *exact* same. Prolly the only nice one
she's got, but she's all acting like that's *who she is*. Like
she's better'n us.

RUTH. Huh.

DONNA. Fake.
What a fake.

(*She returns to her trimming.* **RUTH**'s *attention
stays on Stacia and the office. Beat.*)

RUTH. You know what? I hope she gets it.

(**DONNA** *looks at her.*)

I hope she gets that job, I really do. Why shouldn't she?
What the hell's wrong with her tryna better herself?

Why shouldn't she try workin' in that office instead of down here doin' this shit? If this is the only game in town which it pretty much is, why not get the best job you can out of it?

I mean, I couldn't do it, but if she can, god bless her. That girl and Troy probly'll have some kids soon enough, and that changes things, how you think about your future. I can't blame her. Don't you want your grandkids to have things a little better? What's wrong with her wantin' that?

And you know, come to think of it, so what about her clothes. She came all this way, away from her home and her people to be with Troy, and she don't know anybody and just wants to make a good impression and maybe tried a little too hard. Big whoop, really. What's the alternative, not giving a fuck? That would be better? Why shouldn't she try?

I can't be mad at it.

Good for her.

(*Beat.*)

DONNA. Fuck you, Ruth.

RUTH. 'Scuse me?

DONNA. I mean it, fuck you, fuck the hell out a you. I am so goddamn sick of your attitude, pretending like you are soooo much fuckin' better with your "Oh, I was only on nights for two years because I'm not stupid like everybody else" and "Oh, I coulda worked up in that office" and your big-ass fancy words –

RUTH. What the hell are you talkin' about?

DONNA. – With your "acclimated" and your "aptitude" and your "ergonomics" and your "due deference" you can just go fuck yourself. Because I don't think you even know what half those words mean, you just say 'em 'cause you think they make you sound smart, and that's 'cause that's *the only thing you got*. You don't got any *kids*, you don't got any *husband*, you only landed Henry because he was old and needed somebody to take care of him, you never did have a real man in your goddamn *life* but you like to act like you're so above it all, like you're so much better'n everybody else. You ain't better'n *anybody*, Ruth Thompson. You like to act like you are, it makes you feel better about your shitty life to *think* you are, but you ain't. You ain't shit.

You been actin' like you're better'n me for *twenty fuckin' years* and I AM SICK OF IT.

(**DONNA**, *agitated, is now pointing her shears right at* **RUTH**'s *face.*)

(**RUTH** *looks at the scissors.*)

(*She calmly unhooks her fingers from her own shears and readjusts her grip; she is now holding her pair in her fist. A weapon.*)

(*She looks back up at* **DONNA** *with the cold, dead eyes of a shark. They lock eyes and stare for as long as it takes...*)

(*...For* **DONNA** *to blink first. She looks away and drops her arm. She turns back to the production line and starts cutting away at the backlog of poultry that has stacked up. She works fast, still abuzz with adrenaline.*)

(*Eventually* **RUTH** *returns to her own work. Her movements are calm and controlled.*)

(*She is holding her elbows in.*)

(*They do not look at each other.* **RUTH** *shakes her head.*)

RUTH. Damn, Donna.

(*They work in silence.*)

Goddamn.

(*They continue trimming until the lights fade.*)

End of Play

The Ferberizing
of Coral

Patrick Flynn

THE FERBERIZING OF CORAL was originally produced at CulturalDC's Source Festival (Jenny McConnell Frederick, Artistic Director) in Washington, D.C. on June 12, 2016. The production was dramaturged by Hannah Hessel Ratner and directed by Anne Donnelly. The cast was as follows:

KEVIN . . . . David Johnson

KAREN . . . . Rebecca Ballinger

CORAL AGE 8 & 17 . . . . Emily H. Gilson

KAREN'S MOM . . . . Rebecca Ballinger

KEVIN'S DAD . . . . .Kevin McGuinness

CORAL AGE 33 . . . . Anne Donnelly

THE FERBERIZING OF CORAL was produced as part of the 43rd Annual Samuel French Off Off Broadway Short Play Festival at the Vineyard Theatre in New York City on August 22, 2018. The production was directed by Courtney Laine Self, with sound design by Stephen M. Cyr. The cast was as follows:

KEVIN . . . . Sam Tilles

KAREN . . . . Samm Carroll

CORAL AGE 8 . . . . Clare O'Connell

CORAL AGE 17. . . . . Samm Carroll

KAREN'S MOM / CORAL AGE 33 . . . . .Courtney Laine Self

KEVIN'S DAD . . . . Patrick Flynn

CHARACTERS

KEVIN – a new father
KAREN – a new mother
CORAL (aged **8, 17**, and **33**) – their daughter
KAREN'S MOM
KEVIN'S DAD

SETTING

Living room

TIME

Tonight

AUTHOR'S NOTES

Only the characters of Kevin and Karen appear onstage.
All other characters are only heard through the baby monitor.

(A completely bare stage except for a tasteful end table downstage center with an audio-only baby monitor on it.)

(At rise: **KEVIN** *and* **KAREN** *stand on either side of the table. The lights come up simultaneously with* **KAREN** *turning on the baby monitor. We hear a baby crying.)*

KEVIN. Dammit.

KAREN. Ten minutes.

KEVIN. What does that child want from life?

KAREN. The book says ten minutes so we wait ten minutes.

KEVIN. I'll buy her a fucking car if she'll stop crying.

KAREN. I'll remind her of that when she's old enough to understand what a car is and its value in our society. And stop cursing.

KEVIN. How long now?

KAREN. Ten minutes.

KEVIN. I mean, right now.

KAREN. Nine minutes thirty-seven seconds. Calm down.

KEVIN. She's crawling up my spine.

KAREN. You think I love that sound? You think I love the screams of my infant daughter? But the book says we wait ten minutes so we wait ten minutes. She's got to learn to self-soothe.

KEVIN. Whoever wrote that book is a fucking sadist.

KAREN. Stop cursing. And it worked for the McGeehans.

KEVIN. *Everything* works for the McGeehans. They're fucking superparents.

KAREN. Goddammit stop cursing!

KEVIN. I'm gonna throw the monitor against the...effing wall.

KAREN. Then we wouldn't be able to hear what's effing going on in our daughter's effing room. What if she stopped breathing and we couldn't hear it?

KEVIN. How do you hear someone stop breathing?

(Baby cries louder.)

I'm going in there.

KAREN. You are not.

KEVIN. She's sad. I have the power to make her not sad. It's my only superpower; let me use it.

KAREN. You go in there now and we have to start all over again.

CORAL (8). Daddy? Daddy can you hear me?

KEVIN. Coral?

CORAL (8). Why are you letting me cry, Daddy?

KEVIN. What the fuck is that?

KAREN. Language.

CORAL (8). Mommy?

KAREN. What the eff is that?

KEVIN. Who are you?

CORAL (8). It's me. Coral. Your daughter.

KEVIN. Coral can't talk.

KAREN. Whoever this is, it isn't funny.

CORAL (8). I'm sad and lonely. Why are you letting me cry, Daddy?

KEVIN. Because Mommy is making me.

KAREN. Kevin!

KEVIN. Because some dumb book told us to.

CORAL (8). But I'm sad and alone.

KAREN. You're also a baby. You can't talk yet.

CORAL (8). Now I'm eight and I have a lot of trouble socializing because you let me cry.

KEVIN. It's the future... Our daughter is talking to us from the future. And she's having trouble socializing because we let her cry!

KAREN. That's impossible. And it's for her own good.

CORAL (8). I'm sad, Daddy.

KEVIN. I'm going in.

KAREN. You need to be strong. Stay strong.

CORAL (8). I need you, Mommy.

KAREN. I'm going in.

> (**KEVIN** *stops her.*)

CORAL (8). Mommy? Help me, Mommy.

KEVIN. If I can't go in, you can't go in.

CORAL (8). Daddy? Mommy?

> (*Static comes in over the monitor.*)

KEVIN. We have to stay strong. She can't beat us if we stay strong.

KAREN. You're right. She's fine. It's for her own good.

CORAL (17). Mommy? Why did you let me cry?

KAREN. Coral, you need to go to sleep.

CORAL (17). Now I'm seventeen and I let boys do things to me.

KEVIN. Oh that is effing *it.*

KAREN. Kevin!

KEVIN. Karen, she's seventeen and she's letting boys *do* things to her.

KAREN. No she's not. She is an infant throwing a tantrum.

CORAL (17). I don't know how to love, Mommy. You let me cry and I don't know how to love and I let boys do things to me. In cars.

KEVIN. In *cars,* Karen!

KAREN. Kevin, focus. This is what needs to happen. It's for her own good.

KEVIN. Our parents never did this shit.

KAREN. Yes they did.

KAREN'S MOM. No I didn't.

KAREN. ...Mom?

KAREN'S MOM. Karen, just go pick up my granddaughter.

KAREN. No.

KAREN'S MOM. Karen Elizabeth Montgomery, go in that room and pick up my granddaughter right now. She is sad. Make her not sad.

KEVIN'S DAD. We knew what we were doing. Not like you two.

KEVIN. Dad?

KEVIN'S DAD. Kevin, man up and get your ass in there. You want that sweet, little girl letting boys do things to her? In cars?

KAREN. Kevin and I know what we're doing.

KEVIN'S DAD. Bad enough you named her "Coral."

KEVIN. Dad, we talked about this.

KEVIN'S DAD. Shows a lack of maturity.

KAREN'S MOM. I think it's a nice name.

KAREN. We know what we're doing.

KEVIN. No we don't.

CORAL (33). And now I'm thirty-three alone with cats writing Sherlock Holmes/Doctor Who crossover fan-fiction.

KEVIN. Karen, this is insane. She's our baby. We're the ones who are supposed to take care of her no matter what.

KAREN. This *is* taking care of her.

CORAL (33). I got catfished and lost fifty-six thousand dollars. Twice. All because you let me cry.

KEVIN'S DAD. Back in my day we took care of our children. If they cried and needed to be picked up, we picked them up.

KAREN'S MOM. That's right because we knew what we were doing.

KEVIN. Our parents knew what they were doing, Karen. We're just a couple of idiots who read a book.

KAREN. You said when you were six your dad told you God is always watching.

KEVIN'S DAD. So?

KAREN. *So* he stopped going to the bathroom. He had to be hospitalized.

KEVIN'S DAD. What does that have to do with this? Kevin, go pick up that baby.

KAREN'S MOM. Listen to your elders, Karen.

KAREN. And, Mom, you told me people with mustaches are shifty and not to be trusted.

KEVIN. She did?

KAREN'S MOM. Just go hug the crying baby.

KEVIN'S DAD. What kind of monster lets their own child cry?

KEVIN. They knew what they were doing, Karen, listen to them.

KAREN. How did they know?

KEVIN'S DAD. We just did.

CORAL (8). Save me, Mommy.

KAREN'S MOM. Go pick up your daughter.

KAREN. They made mistakes all the time. They didn't know anything.

KEVIN. They were our parents. They knew things.

KAREN. But how?

CORAL (8). Save me, Mommy. Save me from loneliness.

CORAL (17). Save me from letting boys do things to me in cars.

CORAL (33). Save me from Sherlock Holmes/Doctor Who crossover fan-fiction.

KAREN. Enough!

(She grabs the monitor and turns it off.)

KEVIN. What did you do?

KAREN. I turned it off.

KEVIN. Why did you do that? Give it to me.

KAREN. No.

KEVIN. Give it! *GIVE IT!*

KAREN. I am not effing listening to this anymore. People have been raising children on this planet for millions of years. Coral will be fine.

KEVIN. Give it!

KAREN. Millions of years. And they didn't know any more than we did. They were just like us: assholes. Lazy, grumpy, irresponsible assholes. But they did the best they could with what they had. Millions of years. And they didn't have baby mothers.

KEVIN. Some of them did.

KAREN. Coral will be fine.

KEVIN. How do you know?

KAREN. I don't. But neither did our parents or their parents or their parents.

KEVIN. I / –

KAREN. Coral will be fine. She will soothe herself and come out the other side a strong and defiant woman. And I will be goddammed if I'm going to let my fear beat me. It didn't beat my mom and it won't beat me. Now I'm going to turn this monitor back on and if she's crying, I'm going to turn it off for five minutes then turn it back on again and that's it.

KEVIN. ...I can't do it.

KAREN. But *we* can.

> (*She turns the monitor back on. The light comes on but we hear nothing. She checks the volume but still no sound comes out.*)

KAREN. She's asleep.

> (**KEVIN** *grabs the monitor and fiddles with the volume knob himself.*)

KEVIN. We did it!

> (*They embrace.*)

We survived.

KAREN. We're not bad parents.

KEVIN. We're not.

KAREN. We're good parents.

KEVIN. We're the *best* parents!

KAREN. Our daughter is asleep!

KEVIN. Yes she *is*!

KAREN. ...Unless she's not breathing.

KEVIN. ...She's breathing.

KAREN. How do you know?

KEVIN. I can hear her.

KAREN. You can?

KEVIN. ...No.

KAREN. I'm going up there.

KEVIN. If we open that door, she's going to wake up.

KAREN. Our daughter could be dead!

KEVIN. She's not dead! I'm certain... I'm pretty certain...
I'm fairly certain...

> *(Beat. They dart offstage. Through the monitor
> we hear a door creek open. A baby cries.)*
>
> *(Blackout.)*

End of Play